APR     2007

# Let's Go
# FISHING

Suzanne Slade

**PowerKiDS**
press™

New York

*To Christina, who has always loved to fish and is an awesome angler*

Published in 2007 by The Rosen Publishing Group, Inc.
29 East 21st Street, New York, NY 10010

First Edition

Editor: Amelie von Zumbusch
Book Design: Dean Galiano and Erica Clendening
Layout Design: Julio Gill

Photo Credits: Cover, pp. 10, 22 © Getty Images; p. 4 © www.istockphoto.com/David Lewis; p. 6 U.S. Fish and Wildlife Service. Photo by Bea Schley; p. 7 © www.istockphoto.com/Lawrence Sawyer; p. 8, 26 U.S. Fish and Wildlife Service. Photo by John and Karen Hollingsworth; p. 11 © www.istockphoto.com/Jim Jurica; p. 12 © www.istockphoto.com/Jane Norton; p. 12 (inset) © www.istockphoto.com/Jerry McElroy; p. 14 © www.istockphoto.com/Bill Grove; p. 15 © www.istockphoto.com/Harry Bragdon; p. 16 U.S. Fish and Wildlife Service. Photo by Sherry James; p. 17 U.S. Fish and Wildlife Service. Photo by Robert H. Pos; p. 18 © www.shutterstock.com; p. 20 © National Geographic/Getty Images; p. 21 © www.istockphoto.com/Andrew Howe; p. 24 © www.istockphoto.com/Uli Hamacher; p. 25 U.S. Fish and Wildlife Service. Photo by Eric Engbretson; p. 28 © AFP/Getty.

Library of Congress Cataloging-in-Publication Data

Slade, Suzanne.
  Let's go fishing / Suzanne Slade. — 1st ed.
      p. cm. — (Adventures outdoors)
  Includes bibliographical references and index.
  ISBN-13: 978-1-4042-3647-9 (library binding)
  ISBN-10: 1-4042-3647-3 (library binding)
  1. Fishing—Juvenile literature.  I. Title.
  SH445.S53 2007
  799.1—dc22
                                         2006019562

Manufactured in the United States of America

# Contents

# The Sport of Fishing

People have enjoyed the sport of fishing for thousands of years. The first anglers, or fishermen, fished for food. Today most people go fishing for fun, although some still catch fish to eat. Many enjoy the challenges they must face to find, **attract**, and catch fish. Fishing is a great way to get outside and enjoy nature. Many people like to spend time fishing on a quiet lake with friends.

Fishing is a sport for everyone. People of any age, size, and skill can give fishing a try. You don't need a lot of fancy gear to fish. If you have a simple pole, a worm from your yard, and a nearby river or pond, then you're ready to go fishing!

This boy is fishing from a dock in Ottawa, Ontario.

# Where to Fish

**A** good day of fishing starts with a plan. First you need to choose a place to fish. Most creeks, rivers, lakes, and ponds make good fishing holes. Just be sure to obey any posted No Fishing signs.

Once you arrive at your fishing location, watch for clues to help you find where fish might be hiding. Some fish like to swim near weed beds or reeds. Others can be found in areas of swirling water called

These kids are fishing in the C&O Canal. Canals are another good fishing spot.

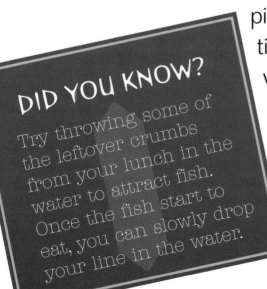

Docks also provide the kind of shaded water in which fish like to hide.

eddies. Fish often stay in shaded water below a tree, pier, or docked boat. If you see tiny air bubbles floating on the water's surface, fish may be eating below. When fishing in a river, look for fish near fast-moving water, such as below a dam or waterfall.

**DID YOU KNOW?**

Try throwing some of the leftover crumbs from your lunch in the water to attract fish. Once the fish start to eat, you can slowly drop your line in the water.

# Fishing Gear

It's helpful to have the right gear and supplies when you go fishing. A fishing trip can last for hours, so take plenty of food and drinks. Wear a hat and sunscreen to keep from getting burned. Sunglasses will protect your eyes and help you find fish in the bright sun. Pack a life jacket that is comfortable and fits properly.

A fishing rod, or pole, is the basic fishing tool you need. Connected to your pole is a reel. A reel is a device that holds a spool of fishing line. Tie a hook on the end of your line and add a metal **sinker** above it. The weight of the sinker will cause your hook and bait to sink in the water. Put a **float** on your line about 1 to 2 feet (.3–.6 m) above your hook to keep your bait from sitting on the bottom of the water.

This boy brought his fishing gear for a trip to California's San Francisco Bay National Wildlife Refuge.

This girl is checking the reel on her fishing rod.

Take a **tackle** box with extra supplies in case your line breaks, a fish steals a hook, or your float drifts away. Bring a sturdy net to land your fish and something to hold your catch. Some people put fish

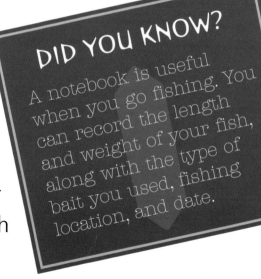

DID YOU KNOW?

A notebook is useful when you go fishing. You can record the length and weight of your fish, along with the type of bait you used, fishing location, and date.

in a wire fishing basket, which they tie to a pier or boat. You can also string your fish on a rope. A large bucket works well, too. Some fishermen have a ruler to measure their fish and a special scale from a tackle store to weigh a prized catch.

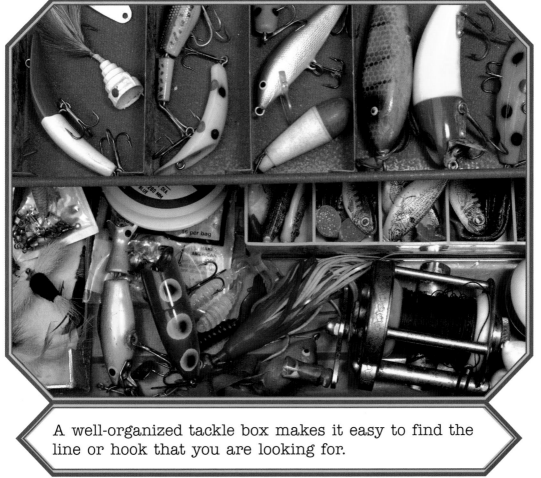

A well-organized tackle box makes it easy to find the line or hook that you are looking for.

# Bait

**A** fisherman uses bait to attract and catch fish. Different kinds of fish like different bait. Whatever bait you use, make sure you push it back on the hook far enough for the sharp end to be visible.

You can use bait you find at home, such as corn, cooked pasta, cheese cubes, bread balls, bologna bits, and jelly beans. Earthworms from your yard also make great bait. A tackle shop sells many kinds of bait, such as red worms, night crawlers, wax worms, and **maggots**. If you are fishing for large fish, you could purchase tiny fish called minnows. Some people use fake fish called lures. Some lures can be tied directly on your line, while others require special gear on your fishing line.

This boy is baiting his hook. *Inset:* Lures come in many different patterns and colors.

# Casting a Line

Casting is the skill of throwing your hook and bait out into the water. There are several kinds of casts, such as underarm casts, beach casts, and overhead casts.

Many anglers use an overhead cast, but make sure the area is clear of wires, trees, and people before you try it. To begin hold your rod over your

You should hold onto your pole with both hands when you are casting.

shoulder at an angle so the hook hangs behind you. Then open the **bale arm** on your reel and press the line coming out of the bale against your rod with a finger. Now quickly push the top end of your rod forward. Take your finger off the line as soon as your rod is pointing toward the water. You will learn the proper timing to cast far with practice.

Always make sure that there is enough open space around you when you are casting.

# Freshwater Fishing

There are many places you can go freshwater fishing. Lakes, rivers, ponds, and small streams are filled with all kinds of delicious freshwater fish. You can fish from the shore, stand in shallow water, or fish off a boat.

Some lakes permit only catch-and-release fishing. Catch-and-release means you put your fish back into

Some people, like the kids above, use a net to fish.

This girl has caught a kind of freshwater fish called a catfish.

the water right after you catch it. This type of fishing protects lakes from running out of fish but still lets anglers enjoy the sport of fishing. It is easier to remove the hook without hurting the fish if you use a barbless hook. This hook does not have a barb, or sharp point located near the end of the hook.

# Fishing in the Ocean

**M**any people enjoy the excitement and challenges of ocean fishing. Whether you go deep-sea fishing on a boat or fish from the beach, you can land some beautiful fish from salt water.

Most fish in the ocean live in deep water. If you are fishing on the beach, you must cast your line far from the shore. You will know a fish is on the line when your float jerks below the water's surface. When a fish bites, pull your pole quickly to **set** the hook. Keep your fishing line tight as you reel in your catch. When the fish arrives at the edge of the water, wait for the next wave to wash it up on the beach.

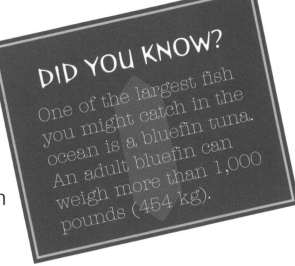

DID YOU KNOW?

One of the largest fish you might catch in the ocean is a bluefin tuna. An adult bluefin can weigh more than 1,000 pounds (454 kg).

Fishing from the shore is called surf casting. Surf casters use especially long fishing poles.

# Fly-Fishing

Fly-fishing is a special type of fishing that's full of action. Fly fishers use a fly made of feathers, hair, and thread for bait. Fish cannot see the hook inside this human-made fly.

Rivers, creeks, streams, ponds, and lakes are great places to fly-fish. To begin you need a special fly rod and reel, a fly line, a **leader**, and a fly. Learning

Fly-fishing takes a lot of practice. This man is fly-fishing in Patagonia, Chile.

Fly-fishing flies are so light that they land gently on the water and fool fish into thinking they are bugs.

to cast your fly requires wide open space and a little patience. An experienced fly fisher can cast a line to an exact location. The fly will appear to dance and move on the surface of the water, making it look like a tasty insect. With some luck a hungry fish will strike, or bite the fly.

**DID YOU KNOW?**

There are thousands of kinds of flies. You can buy flies in many different shapes, sizes, and weights. Some people enjoy making their own flies.

# Ice Fishing

**S**ome people fish through a hole on a frozen lake. This is called ice fishing. You can ice fish when it has been very cold for long periods of time. Ice must be at least 4 inches (10 cm) thick before it is safe to walk and fish on. You can use a spud to cut holes in ice. A spud is a metal bar with a blade at one end. A hole larger than 8 inches (20 cm) is a good size for ice fishing.

An ice-fishing rod is shorter than a regular pole. The short length allows you to sit close to your hole and watch for fish on the line. Ice fishing lets people enjoy the sport of fishing all year long.

Ice fishermen must wear plenty of clothes, heavy boots, and gloves to stay warm.

# Kinds of Fish

There are many types of fish you can catch for sport or food. People often eat freshwater fish such as perch, bluegill, bass, trout, and salmon. Perch are round and narrow. They often swim in groups and like shady areas. Bluegills are wider and more

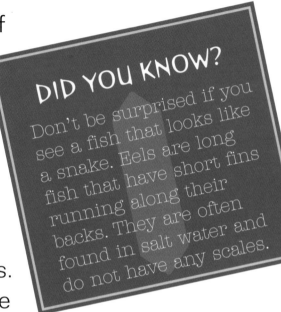

Rainbow trout live west of the Rocky Mountains. They are also known as redband trout and steelhead.

colorful. You may spot them in shallow water. Perch and bluegill are easily caught with earthworms. Bass are a large, brownish fish that prefer deeper water. An **artificial** worm or lure attracts bass. Fishermen find trout and salmon in rivers.

The vast ocean holds many unusual fish. In the Southeast, grouper is popular. Flounder and sole live on the east and west coasts. These fish swim near the sea floor, so your bait must be placed low to catch them.

Sole live on the ocean floor. Adult sole have both of their eyes on the same side of their head.

# Fishing and Nature

**F**ish are a source of food and sport for people all over the world. In certain areas pollution causes some fish to be unsafe to eat and others to die. **Conservationists** work to teach people how to keep lakes and rivers clean. As **overfishing** and pollution reduce the fish population, workers may **stock** some lakes with more fish.

Special fish farms called fisheries have large tanks for raising fish. This is one way to provide people with clean fish to eat. In a fishery people can carefully control the water quality along with the food that the fish eat. By working with nature, we can help keep the fish population safe and plentiful.

This scientist from the U.S. Fish and Wildlife Service is preparing to restock fish in Piedmont, Georgia.

# Let's Go Fishing!

**F**ishing is a great sport that helps you enjoy nature. Anyone can fish with a simple pole and hook. To learn more about the sport, you can practice a new skill or try new gear.

Some people like to test their skills in a fishing **tournament**. Some tournaments last a few hours, and others last for days. Everyone in a fishing contest must catch the same type of fish. The person who catches the largest fish wins a prize, such as money, fishing gear, or a new boat. Winning prizes is fun, but any fisherman will tell you the best prize of all is the thrill of reeling in your own fish.

So what are you waiting for? Grab your pole and let's go fishing!

This angler is showing off the huge sailfish he caught in a fishing tournament in the Philippines.

# Safety Tips

- Don't go fishing by yourself. Always take a buddy with you.

- Wear a life jacket while you fish.

- When you go fishing, stay away from overhead electrical lines. Your rod can conduct electricity.

- Don't leave trash, old fishing line, or hooks behind after you fish. Animals can be hurt if they become tangled in line or eat or step on hooks.

- Stand on firm ground or a surface that is not slippery when you fish.

- Look carefully around you to make sure the area is clear before you cast your line.

- Don't fish in water that looks polluted.

- Some fish have teeth or sharp fins. Have an adult help you handle these fish or use a cloth to hold them safely.

- Have an adult help you clean your fish. Be especially careful when using sharp knives.

- Fish have a lot of small bones. When you eat fish, watch carefully for bones and eat slowly so you don't choke.

# Glossary

**artificial** (ar-tih-FIH-shul) Made by people, not nature.

**attract** (uh-TRAKT) To cause people, animals, or things to want to be near you.

**bale arm** (BAYL AHRM) A spinning arm on a fishing pole that winds line onto a spool.

**conservationists** (kon-ser-VAY-shun-ists) People who want to protect nature.

**float** (FLOHT) Something that rests on top of water.

**leader** (LEE-der) The fine line that connects the fly to the fishing line.

**maggots** (MA-guts) Small, legless baby insects.

**overfishing** (oh-ver-FISH-ing) Catching too many fish.

**set** (SET) To fix a hook in a fish's mouth.

**sinker** (SIN-ker) A weight used to sink fishing lines or nets.

**stock** (STOK) To refill the supply of something.

**tackle** (TA-kul) Having to do with the gear and tools used for a sport or hobby.

**tournament** (TOR-nuh-ment) A contest.

# Index

**A**
bait, 9, 13–14, 20
bale arm, 15

**C**
conservationists, 27

**F**
float, 9–10, 19
food, 5, 9, 24, 27

**G**
gear, 5, 9, 29

**H**
hook, 9–10, 13–14, 17, 19–20

**L**
leader, 20
line, 9–10, 13, 15, 19–21, 23
lure(s), 13

**M**
maggots, 13

**O**
overfishing, 27

**P**
pole, 5, 9, 23, 29. *See also* rod
pollution, 27

**R**
reel, 9, 15, 20
rod, 9, 14–15, 20, 23. *See also* pole

**S**
sinker, 9
supplies, 9–10

**T**
tackle box, 10
tournament, 29

**W**
worm(s), 5, 13, 25

# Web Sites

Due to the changing nature of Internet links, PowerKids Press has developed an online list of Web sites related to this book. This site is updated regularly. Please use this link to access the list:
www.powerkidslinks.com/adout/fishing/